to Hanna from Grandma
Christmas 1994

to Hanna from Grandma
Christmas 1994

THE KING WHO SNEEZED

For Georgia and Bobje AM
For Mum and Dad SH

THE KING WHO SNEEZED

Written by Angela McAllister   Illustrated by Simon Henwood

Morrow Junior Books
New York

Once upon a time, in a country so far north that it was always winter, there ruled a mean and stingy King called Parsimonious.

His ancient castle high up in the Drafty Mountains was crumbling away because the stingy King would not have the rotten roofs repaired or the damp dungeons drained. All year the castle was shivery cold but King Parsimonious would not buy any firewood.

Instead, he wore a woolly hat, a stripy scarf that went round three times, two pairs of thick football socks and his fleecy-lined mittens. Sometimes he even kept hot potatoes in his pockets. When he wasn't on his throne he stayed in bed with the Royal Hot Water Bottle and a flask of tea.

All the King's Men kept their woolly vests on every day (except the first of June when they went in the wash).

Every day at noon the King always had his favorite meal of green alphabetti spaghetti with a cheese and onion milk shake and chocolate peppermint jelly with mustard sauce. And every day he complained that the alphabetti spaghetti wasn't hot enough.

"Thundering Thimbles! How can I ever get warm if my dinner is cold?" he bellowed at the cooks.

All the cooks grumbled that there was nothing they could do – the meal always got cold on its chilly journey from the kitchen to the Throne Room.

One day as he took his first bite of green alphabetti
spaghetti, King Parsimonious felt an icy wind poke its
freezing fingers down his neck.

"Galligaskins!" shouted the King. "Where's this draft
coming from?"

But nobody answered him. It was the Official Afternoon
Off and All the King's Men had just left to visit their friends
in warm castles, where there were crackling log fires and
hot dragon noodle soup.

The draft wriggled further down the King's neck.
Suddenly he sneezed and an icicle froze on his nose.
"Botherations!" he said. "I will have to see to that draft
myself and warm up my own food."

As everyone knows, it is difficult to walk in two pairs of
thick football socks, carrying a plate of green alphabetti
spaghetti, especially if your teeth are chattering, your knees
are knocking and your hands are numb with cold, but
slowly King Parsimonious shuffled through the castle.

The King eventually found himself at the door of the dark cellar. Peering over the top of his scarf, he could just see a thin light and smell a bold blast of icy air, so, nervously, he stepped inside. Sure enough, there was the back door of the castle left open and the wintry wind was whistling through.

"Marrowbones and Cleavers!" The King tried to shut the heavy door. He heaved with his hands and he shoved with his shoulders; he bumped with his bottom and he hammered with his head. The door wouldn't budge. Exhausted, he sat down on the cold stone floor and bashed his elbow on something in the doorway.

"Jumping Jellyfish! The Royal Doorstop!"

The King pulled it out and, with a tap of his little finger, the heavy door shut with a thud.

As everyone knows, it is difficult to walk in two pairs of thick football socks, carrying a plate of green alphabetti spaghetti, when your teeth are chattering, your knees knocking and your hands are numb with cold – IN THE DARK – but, slowly, King Parsimonious shuffled out of the cellar.

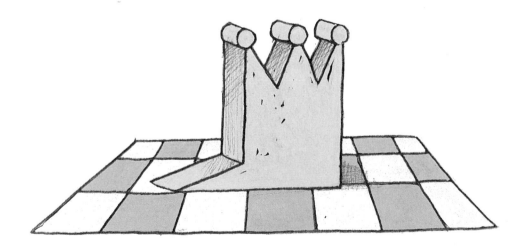

"At last, no more drafts in the castle," the King said to himself. But suddenly he felt a sneeze coming on – yes, no . . . yes . . . no . . . no . . . er . . . "T'shoo!" And an icicle froze on the Royal Nose. Another draft, chillier than the last, was rushing along the hall.

So, through the hall and down the tower steps, the King followed the draft until he finally came to the castle kitchen. Through the kitchen and down a spiral staircase, the King finally came to the Royal Pantry and there was the pantry window WIDE OPEN!

"Popguns and Penny whistles!" The King tried to force the stubborn window shut. He pressed it down but the wind thrust it up. He pushed it in but the wind gusted it out. He slammed it forward but the wind blasted it backward. Suddenly the latch snapped off with a *ping* and landed in an empty milk bottle. And there on the windowsill the King saw ten bottles.

"Jackdaws and Junket!"

The King brought the bottles inside and lined them up to wedge the window shut.

"At last, no more drafts in the castle!" the King said to himself, satisfied. "Now I can warm up my dinner."

As everyone knows, it is difficult to walk in two pairs of thick football socks, carrying a plate of green alphabetti spaghetti, with your teeth chattering, your knees knocking and your hands numb with cold, in the dark, down the stairs – but it is even harder TO GO UPSTAIRS. Slowly, King Parsimonious shuffled up to the kitchen.

But when he got to the top step he had a feeling . . . he suddenly knew . . . he thought he knew . . . he wasn't sure . . . er . . . "T'shoo!" Two icicles froze on the Royal Nose – and a perishing draft nipped his toes and turned them blue.

Looking down, the King saw two big holes in his socks. Another draft, even chillier than the last, was whistling across the kitchen floor.

"Fishcakes and Frying pans!" roared the King, and he dropped his plate of green alphabetti spaghetti.

By now it was dark inside and outside. King
Parsimonious searched for the draft but he walked
straight into the kitchen cupboard, cracked his nose and sat
down with a bump! And there was the raw wind at his feet,
shooting through the Royal Cat Flap.

"Windmills and Wheelbarrows!" he bellowed. Hard as he
tried to shut the flap, the wind rattled it open, for there was
nothing to hold it closed.

In the corner of the kitchen was a huge sack of dried beans. The King tried to push it toward the Cat Flap. He dragged and dragged until he was so warm that he took off his mittens; he heaved and heaved until he was so warm that he took off his scarf; he kicked and kicked until he was so warm that he took off his socks. Exhausted, he rested against the sack and, with a clatter, the beans spilled out into a huge pile against the Cat Flap.

"At last, no more drafts in the castle," the King said to himself, finally satisfied. But as he brushed the beans from his lap he had a sudden feeling . . . no, not again . . . not another one . . . no more sneezes . . . ah . . . ah . . . "Aaahhh!" The King yawned. He felt tired and warm.

As everyone knows, it takes only two minutes to find your bedchamber when you are feeling warm and tired, and soon King Parsimonious was tucked up fast asleep – without the Royal Hot Water Bottle.

But when the King woke up the next morning, he felt as cold as ever, and even grumpier when he remembered that he hadn't had his meal the day before.

"Inkwells and Icebergs ! It's so chilly I shall stay in bed all day."

He sent for All the King's Men and for the castle cooks, who shivered and shuffled into his bedchamber.

"Bring my scarf and socks and mittens, the Royal Hot Water Bottle, a flask of tea and bring my meal, now, and make it hot!"

Everything arrived except the meal. The King waited impatiently. He didn't see the cooks shaking nervously outside his door.

"You take it in."

"No, go on, you take it in."

"Not me, you take it in."

Eventually, the smallest, youngest cook was pushed into the bedchamber with the Royal Dinner Tray.

"SHOEHORNS AND SHUTTLECOCKS! WHAT HAPPENED TO MY FOOD!" roared the King in a red rage.

For there on the Dinner Tray was a raspberry jam sandwich and a custard cream bun!

"Where's my green alphabetti spaghetti with a cheese and onion milk shake and chocolate peppermint jelly with mustard sauce?"

"YourMajestyMostHighnessKingshipSir," the poor cook whimpered, "somebody shut the cellar door – and the spaghetti got damp and moldy."

"Oh . . . er . . . did it?" The King's red rage changed to a pink blush. "What about my cheese and onion milk shake?"

"Your MajestyMostHighnessKingnessSir, somebody shut the pantry window so the milkman couldn't leave the milk. And somebody spilt the beans in front of the Cat Flap so the Royal Cat could not come in to chase the rats – and they ate all the cheese."

"Oh . . . er . . . they did, did they? And I suppose the rats ate all the chocolate, too?"

"No, Your Majesty, we had to call for the rat catcher and HE ate all the chocolate."

"Crumbling Christmas Cakes!"

"You see," the smallest, youngest cook explained, "we must have the doors and windows open for your food but it is so very, very COLD . . ." And he shivered and sneezed loudly, which reminded the King of the freezing North Wind and its drafty fingers. The King shuddered. Then suddenly he jumped out of bed.

"Gusty Gales and Glaciers! Here is a proclamation: Starting this morning, we shall repair the roofs, drain out the dungeons and send for supplies of candles and firewood. So from this day, there will never be another sneeze heard in the castle again!"

When all the work was done, King Parsimonious put his woolly hat, his stripy scarf, his thick football socks and his fleecy-lined mittens away in the cupboard and only put them on again when he went out for snowball fights.

All the woolly vests were thrown out and All the King's
Men had their friends to the castle for tea.
   The cooks spent every day happily inventing wonderful
new hot dishes for the King and singing, as happy cooks do.

With all the warm fires, jolly teatimes, and cooks singing, King Parsimonious didn't feel mean anymore. He wore only slippers, a dressing-gown and a Royal Smile. And there was nothing that made him smile more than to sit with his friend the smallest, youngest cook, eating hot buttered toast in front of a roaring fire, watching the North Wind press its icy nose against the window.

"Hearthrugs and Hot pots." The happy King laughed. "YOU CAN'T COME IN!"

Printed in Italy.
1 2 3 4 5 6 7 8 9 10
Library of Congress Cataloging-in-Publication Data
McAllister, Angela.
The king who sneezed/Angela McAllister
illustrations by Simon Henwood. p.   cm.
Summary: Mean and stingy King Parsimonious does not care about the
comfort of his subjects until he tries to find out why his castle
is so cold and makes some interesting discoveries about his
household.
ISBN 0-688-08327-7.   ISBN 0-688-08328-5   (lib. bdg.)
[1. Kings, queens, rulers, etc.—Fiction.   2. Castles—Fiction.
3. Cold—Fiction.   4. Generosity—Fiction.]   I. Henwood, Simon,
ill.   II. Title.
PZ7.M11714Ki   1988
[E]—dc 19   88-6858   CIP   AC